DUBS

GOES TO

WASHINGTON

Dick Morris · Eileen McGann · Clayton Liotta

Illustrations by Clayton Liotta

Requests for permission to make copies of any part of the work should be submitted online at info@velocity-press.com or mailed to Velocity Press, Suite 1000, 49 Twin Lakes Road, South Salem, NY 10590.

Library of Congress Cataloging-in-Publication Data is pending.

Printed in the United States of America.

ISBN: 978-1-938804-07-6

www.velocity-press.com

Velocity Press

Here are some other books I've written as part of my
DUBS DISCOVERS AMERICA series:

Dubs Runs for President

and

Dubs Goes to Philadelphia

Dubs took a train to Washington
To see his country's sights,
And play with his tennis ball
In which he just delights.
But when the train pulled into
The station at D.C.,
The ball rolled away
To where Dubs couldn't see.

The ball rolled faster and faster,
It was a total disaster,
Because it did not stop or slow down,
And poor Dubs had to look for it
All over Washington town.

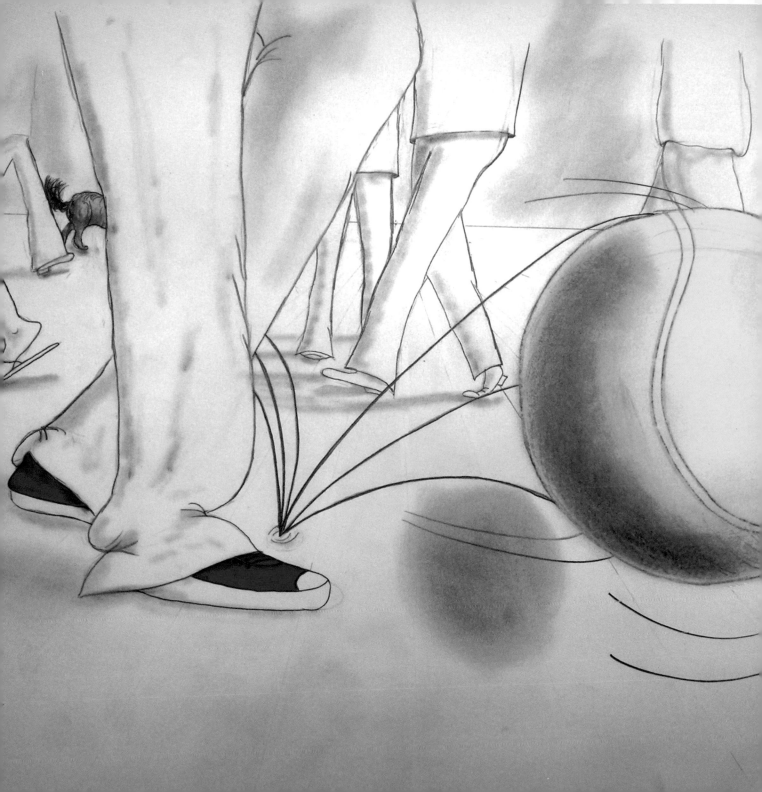

At the memorial for Abraham Lincoln,
Dubs sat up and started thinkin':
If man from chains is meant to be free,
Will someone take this silly leash off of me!

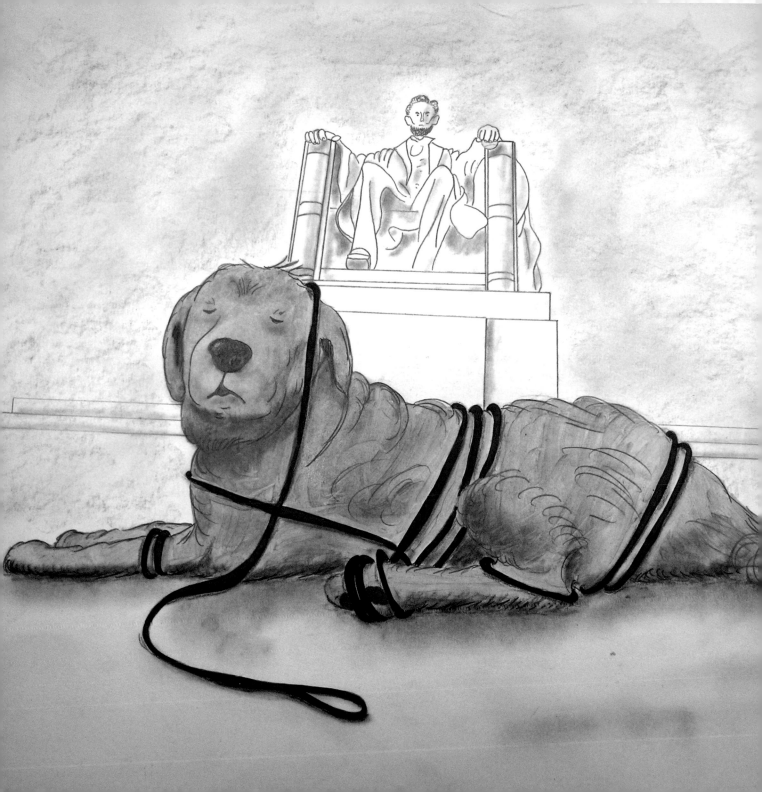

George Washington was president number one,
Back when our country had just begun.
His monument stands straight and tall,
And excuse me while I search for my ball.

In front of the U.S. Supreme Court
Dubs had an important thought:
If another dog took away my ball,
The Court would get it back for me after all.

At the Smithsonian they have the rockets
That went off into space,
Which is very dark and lonely
And a great big empty place.
They show the men who walked
On the face of the rocky moon.
Do you think that dogs can do that
Anytime soon?

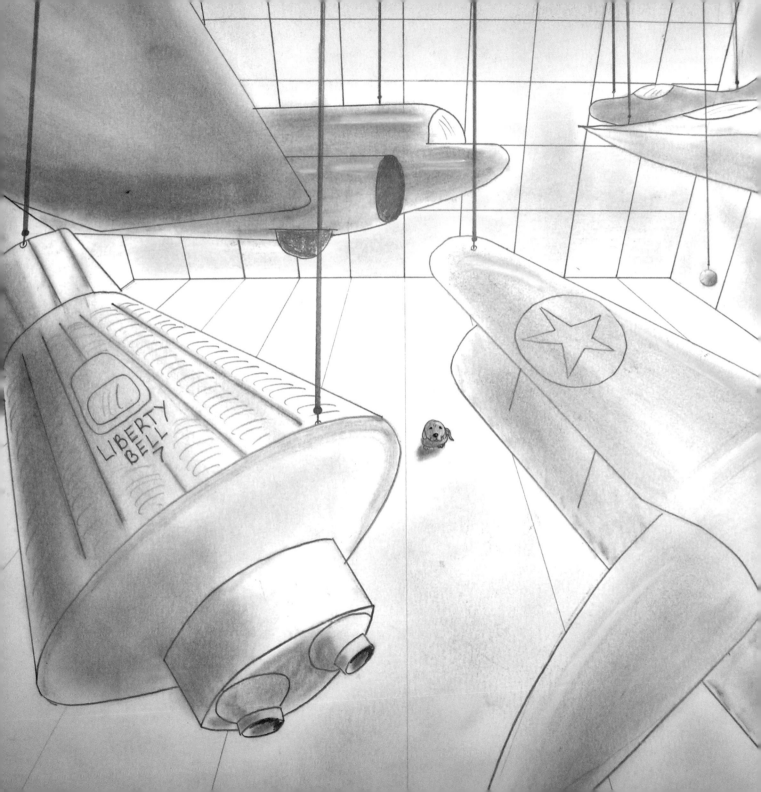

Our flag was planted by the U.S. Marines,
In one of our history's most famous scenes.

To the troops who made sure
That freedom never fails,
People give thanks
And dogs wag their tails.

"I have a dream,"
Martin Luther King once said,
Throughout the long march for equality
That he so bravely led.

Skin color makes no difference,
This I can plainly see.
I love *everyone* who throws a ball
To my pals and then to me.

Here's where Congress meets
To pass laws and spend our money.
The Capitol police were there in force
And did not think it funny
When I ran up and down
This building's famous hall,
Looking all over the place
For my lost and missing ball.

Here's where all our coins are made,
They say that they are "minted,"
This is the place where America's money
Is designed and nicely printed.
They keep the dollars in these big piles
So tall but oh, so neat.
And they could buy more tasty biscuits
Than even Dubs could eat.

The G-men are the agents
Of the famous FBI,
Who catch all of the bad guys
On land and sea and sky.
And when a person goes missing,
They give the case their all.
Hey, do you think it might be possible
For these guys to find my ball?

At the White House in the springtime
Kids hunt for Easter eggs.
Dubs joined them in the hunt and ran
Between the president's legs.
He looked up at the president,
Who stood so big so tall.
But he didn't want to find an egg,
He wanted to find his ball.

Dubs came to the statue of FDR,
One of our greatest presidents by far.

He led us to victory in World War Two
And had a dog named Fala, who Dubs never knew.

At the memorial for the Second World War,
Dubs was thrilled by what he saw.

The monuments were to those who kept us free,
But still there was no ball that he could see.

The Library of Congress has every book,
So Dubs decided to have a look.
The ball wasn't in the section on pets or sports.
Dubs was getting somewhat out of sorts!

"All men are created equal,"
Thomas Jefferson famously wrote
In the Declaration of Independence's
Most often quoted quote.

If people are equal, can it possibly be
That dogs are too . . . especially me?

At the Tomb of the Unknown Soldier
We honor heroes past.
Dubs thought that in this solemn place
He'd find his ball at last.
Just then a man in uniform
Came walking Dubs' way.
And it was clear to one and all
That he had something important to say.

"I've served our country in peace and in war
And I love America but I'll say no more.
Say, is this the ball you've been looking for?"

I've got my ball! Hip hip hooray!
But more important
Is what I've learned today.

America is great
And brave and free,
And a wonderful home
For you and for me!

Back on the train
Dubs started to smile,
And looked at the countryside
For quite a while.
He thought, "No matter how far I roam,
This is America.
My home sweet home!"

Dear Reader:

I hope you enjoyed reading about Washington, D.C. I had to work hard to find my lost ball, but I'm glad I did because it took me to many fun places, and I learned some interesting things about our nation's capital.

When you have time, draw something on the inside of the front and back covers that reminds you of Washington. Try the Washington Monument. It's the tallest building in the city. The law says nothing can be higher.

If you have not seen my other books, you might want to take a look. After my visit to D.C., I decided to run for office myself in a book called DUBS RUNS FOR PRESIDENT. What a crazy time that was, running against Felix the Cat! Guess who won? You'll be surprised how that came out.

After that, I went to Philadelphia, the City of Brotherly Love where our Constitution was created. Look for me and my pal, Daisy, in DUBS GOES TO PHILADELPHIA.

To tell me what you think about my adventures, or anything else you want me to know, email me at Dubs@DubsTheDog.com or visit me at Facebook.com/DubsTheDog. And don't forget: I'm a Golden Retriever! I love you guys!

Okay, time to take a nap. I sleep on a porch, how about you?

Your pal,
Dubs

USE THIS PAGE FOR
PICTURES, DRAWINGS,
AND YOUR PET'S PAW PRINTS